HORRID HENRY
ROBS THE BANK

Meet HORRID HENRY
the laugh-out-loud
worldwide sensation!

* Over 15 million copies sold in 27 countries and counting

* # 1 chapter book series in the UK

* Francesca Simon is the only American author to ever win the Galaxy British Book Awards Children's Book of the year (past winners include J. K. Rowling, Philip Pullman, and Eoin Colfer).

"I have tried out the Horrid Henry books with groups of children as a parent, as a babysitter, and as a teacher. **Children love to either hear them read aloud or to read them themselves**." —Danielle Hall, teacher

"A flicker of recognition must pass through most teachers and parents when they read Horrid Henry. **There's a tiny bit of him in all of us**." —Nancy Astee, *Child Education*

"**As a teacher...it's great to get a series of books my class loves**. They go mad for Horrid Henry." —teacher

"**Short, easy-to-read chapters will appeal to early readers, who will laugh at Henry's exaggerated antics and relate to his rambunctious personality**." —*School Library Journal*

"AN absolutely faNtaStic SerieS aNd Surely a wiNNer with all childreN. LoNg live FraNceSca SimoN aNd her brilliaNt bookS! More, more pleaSe!" —pareNt

"**Laugh-out-loud reading for both adults and children alike**." —parent

"**Henry's over-the-top behavior, the characters" snappy dialogue, and Ross's hyperbolic line art will engage even the most reluctant readers—there's little reason to suspect the series won't conquer these shores as well**." —*Publishers Weekly*

Horrid Henry by Francesca Simon

HORRID HENRY
ROBS THE BANK

Francesca Simon
Illustrated by Tony Ross

sourcebooks
jabberwocky

Text © Francesca Simon 2008
Cover and internal illustrations © Tony Ross 2008
Cover and internal design © 2013 by Sourcebooks, Inc.

Published by Sourcebooks Jabberwocky, an imprint of Sourcebooks, Inc.
P.O. Box 4410, Naperville, Illinois 60567-4410
(630) 961-3900
Fax: (630) 961-2168
www.jabberwockykids.com

Originally published in Great Britain in 2008 by Orion Children's Books.

Library of Congress Cataloging-in-Publication data is on file with the publisher.

Source of Production: Versa Press, East Peoria, Illinois, USA
Date of Production: April 2015
Run Number: 5003577

Printed and bound in the United States of America.
VP 10 9 8 7 6 5 4 3

For my brilliant friend Dina Rabinovitch,
who did so much for children's literature,
and for her son, Elon Julius

CONTENTS

1

HORRID HENRY'S NEWSPAPER

"It's not fair!" howled Horrid Henry. "I want a Hip-Hop Robot dog!"

Horrid Henry needed money. Lots and lots and lots of money. His parents didn't need money, and yet they had tons more than he did. It was so unfair. Why was he so brilliant at *spending* money, and so bad at *getting* money?

And now Mom and Dad refused to buy him something he desperately needed.

"You have plenty of toys," said Mom.

"Which you never play with," said Dad.

"That's 'cause they're all so boring!" screeched Henry. "I want a robot dog!"

"Too expensive," said Mom.

"Too noisy," said Dad.

"But *everyone* has a Hip-Hop Robot Dog," whined Henry. "Everyone but *me*."

Horrid Henry stomped out of the room. How could he get some money?

Wait. Maybe he could *persuade* Peter to give him some. Peter always had tons of cash because he never bought anything.

Yes! He could hold Peter's Bunnykins for ransom. He could tell Peter his room

was haunted and get Peter to pay him for ghostbusting. He could make Peter donate to Henry's favorite charity, Child in Need… Hip-Hop Robot Dog, here I come, thought Horrid Henry, bursting into Peter's bedroom.

Perfect Peter and Tidy Ted were whispering together on the floor. Papers were scattered all around them.

"You can't come in my room," said Peter.

"Yes I can," said Henry, "'cause I'm already in. Pooh, your room stinks."

"That's 'cause you're in it," said Peter.

Henry decided to ignore this insult. "Whatcha doing?"

"Nothing," said Peter.

"We're writing our own newspaper like Mrs. Oddbod suggested in assembly," said Ted. "We've even got a *Tidy with Ted* column," he added proudly.

"A snooze paper, you mean," said Henry.

"It is not," said Peter.

Henry snorted. "What's it called?"

"*The Best Boys' Busy Bee*," said Peter.

"What a stupid name," said Henry.

"It's not a stupid name," said Peter. "Miss Lovely said it was perfect."

"Peter, I have a great idea for your paper," said Henry.

"What?" said Peter cautiously.

"You can use your newspaper for Fluffy's litter box."

"MOOOM!" wailed Peter. "Henry's being mean to me."

"Don't be horrid, Henry!" shouted Mom.

"Peter is a poopsicle, Peter is a poopsicle," chanted Henry.

But then Peter did something strange. Instead of screaming for Mom, Peter started writing.

"Now everyone who buys my newspaper will know how horrid you are," said Peter, putting down his pencil.

Buy? *Buy?*

"We're selling it in school tomorrow," said Ted. "Miss Lovely said we could."

Sell? *Sell?*

"Lemme see that," said Henry, yanking the paper out of Peter's hands.

The *Busy Bee's* headline read:

PETER IN THE GOOD AS GOLD BOOK FOR THE FOURTH TIME THIS MONTH

Horrid Henry snorted. What a worm. Then his eye caught the second headline:

COMPUTER BAN FOR HORRID BOY

Henry was banned from playing games on the computer today because he was mean to his brother Peter and called him wibble pants and poopsicle. *The Busy Bee* hopes Henry has learned his lesson and will stop being such a big meanie.

"You're going to…*sell* this?" spluttered Henry. His name would be mud. Worse than mud. Everyone would know what a stupid toad brother he had. Worse, some people might even *believe* Peter's lies.

And then suddenly Horrid Henry had a brilliant, spectacular idea. He'd write his *own* newspaper. Everyone would want to buy it. He'd be rich!

He could call his newspaper *The Hourly Howler* and charge 25¢ a copy. If he could write seven editions a day, and sell each copy to 500 people, he'd make... he'd make...well, multiplication was never his best subject, but he could make *tons* of money!!!!!!

On the other hand, writing seven newspapers a day, every day, seemed an awful lot of work. An awful, awful lot of work. Perhaps *The Daily Digger* was the way to go. He'd charge a lot more per copy, and do a lot less work. Yes!

Hmmn. Perhaps *The Weekly Warble* would be better. No, *The Monthly Moaner*.

Maybe just *The Purple Hand Basher*.

The Basher! What a great name for a great paper!

Now, what should his newspaper have? News of course. All about Henry's triumphs. And gossip and quizzes and sports.

First, I need a great headline, thought Horrid Henry.

What about: PETER IS A WORM. Tempting, thought Henry, but old news: everyone already knows that

8

Peter is a worm. What could he tell his readers that they *didn't* know?

After all, news didn't have to be true, did it? Just *new*. And boy did he have some brand-new news!

PETER SENT TO PRISON

The world's toadiest brother has been found guilty of being a worm and taken straight to prison. He was sentenced to live on bread and water for three years. *The Basher* says: "It should have been ten years."

SECRET CLUB COLLAPSES!!!

The Secret Club has collapsed. "Margaret is such a moody old bossy-pants no one wants to be in her club anymore," said Susan.

"Goodbye, grump-face," said Gurinder.

Right, that was the news section taken care of. Now, for some good gossip.

But what gossip? What scandal? Sadly, Horrid Henry didn't know any horrid rumors. But a gossip columnist needed to write something…

MRS. ODDBOD BIKINI SHOCK

Mrs. Oddbod was
seen strolling
down Main Street
wearing a new
yellow polka dot
bikini. Is this any
way for a principal
to behave?

TEACHER IN
TOILET TERROR

Terrible screams rang out from the boys'
bathroom yesterday. "Help! Help! There's a
monster in the toilet!" screamed the crazed
teacher Miss Boudicca Battle-Axe. "It's got
hairy scary claws and three heads!!"

GUESS WHO?

Which soggy swimming teacher was seen dancing the cha-cha-cha with which old battle-axe?

MISS LOVELY IN NOSE PICK HORROR

Oh dear, Miss Lydia Lovely picks her nose.

"I saw her do it in class," says Prisoner Peter.

"But she said it was her nose and she would pick it if she wanted to."

THE NURSE HAS LICE!

Nitty Nora, Bug Explorer was sent home from school with lice last week. Whoopee! No more bug-busting!

That's enough great gossip for one issue, thought Horrid Henry. Now, what else, what else? A bit about sports and he was done. In tomorrow's edition, he'd add a comic strip: The adventures of Peter the Diaper. And a quiz:

Who has the smelliest pants in school?
A. Peter
B. Margaret
C. Susan
D. All of the above!

Yippee! thought Horrid Henry. I'm going to be rich, rich, rich, rich, rich.

The next morning Henry made sure he got to school bright and early. Hip-hop Robot, here I come, thought Horrid Henry, lugging a huge pile of *Bashers* onto the playground. Then he stopped.

A terrible sight met his eyes.

Moody Margaret and Sour Susan were standing in the school playground waving big sheets of paper.

"Step right up, read all about it, Margaret made captain of the school soccer team," bellowed Moody Margaret. "Get your *Daily Dagger* right here. Only 25 cents!"

What a copycat, thought Horrid Henry. He was outraged.

"Who'd want to read *that*?" sneered Horrid Henry.

"Everyone," said Susan.

Horrid Henry snatched a copy.

"That'll be 25 cents, Henry," said Margaret.

Henry ignored her. The headline read:

MARGARET TRIUMPHS

Margaret, the best soccer player in school

history, beat out her puny opposition to become captain of the school soccer team! Well done Margaret! Everyone cheered for hours when Mrs. Oddbod announced the glorious news.

Margaret gave an exclusive interview to the **Daily Dagger**:

"It's hard being as amazing as I am," said Margaret. "So many people are jealous, especially stinky pants pimples like Henry."

"What a load of garbage," said Horrid Henry, scrunching up Margaret's newspaper.

"Our customers don't think so," said Margaret. "I'm making *tons* of loot. Before you know it *I'll* have the first Hip-Hop Robot Dog. And you–ooooo won't," she chanted.

"We'll see about that," said Horrid Henry. "Teacher in toilet terror! Read all about it!" he hollered. "All the news and gossip. Only 25 cents."

"News! News!" screeched Margaret. "Step right up, step right up! Only 24 cents."

"Buy the *Busy Bee*!" piped Peter. "Only 5 cents."

Rude Ralph bought a *Basher*. So did Dizzy Dave and Jolly Josh.

Lazy Linda approached Margaret.

"Oy, Linda, don't buy that rubbish," shouted Henry. "*I've* got the best news and gossip." Henry whispered in Linda's ear. Her jaw dropped and she handed Henry a quarter.

"Don't listen to him!" squealed Margaret.

"Buy the *Busy Bee*," trilled Perfect Peter. "Free vegetable chart."

"Margaret, did you see what Henry wrote about you?" gasped Gorgeous Gurinder.

"What?" said Margaret, grabbing a *Basher*.

SPORTS
SHOCKING SOCCER NEWS

There was shock all around when Henry wasn't made captain of the school soccer team.

"It's an outrage," said Dave.

"Disgusting," said Soraya.

The Basher was lucky enough to get an exclusive interview with Henry.

"Not making me captain just goes to show what an idiot that old carrot-nose Miss Battle-Axe is," says Henry.

The Basher says: **Make Henry captain**!

"What!" screamed Margaret. "Dave and Soraya never said *that*."

"They thought it," said Henry. He glared at Moody Margaret.

Moody Margaret glared at Horrid Henry.

Henry's hand reached out to pull Margaret's hair.

Margaret's foot reached out to kick Henry's leg.

Suddenly Mrs. Oddbod walked onto the playground. There was a stern-looking man with her, wearing a suit and carrying a notebook. Miss Battle-Axe and Miss Lovely followed.

Aha, new customers, thought Horrid Henry, as they headed toward him.

"Get your school paper here!" hollered Henry. "Only 50 cents."

"News! News!" screeched Margaret. "Step right up, step right up! 49 cents."

"Buy the *Busy Bee!*" trilled Peter. "Only 5 cents."

"Well, well," said the strange man. "What have we here, Mrs. Oddbod?"

Mrs. Oddbod beamed. "Just three of our best students showing how enterprising they are," she said.

Horrid Henry thought his ears had fallen off. *Best* student? And why was Mrs. Oddbod smiling at him? Mrs. Oddbod *never* smiled at him.

"Peter, why don't you tell the inspector what you're doing," said Miss Lovely.

"I've written my own newspaper to raise money for the school," said Perfect Peter.

"Very impressive, Mrs. Oddbod," said the school inspector, smiling. "Very impressive. And what about you, young man?" he added, turning to Henry.

"I'm selling my newspaper for a Child in Need," said Horrid Henry. In need of a Hip-Hop Robot, he thought. "How many do you want to buy?"

The school inspector handed over 50¢ and took a paper.

"I love school newspapers," he said, starting to read. "You find out so much

about what's really happening at a
school."

The school inspector gasped. Then he
turned to Mrs. Oddbod.

"What do you know about a yellow
polka dot bikini?" said the Inspector.

"Yellow…polka…dot…bikini?" said
Mrs. Oddbod.

"Cha-cha-cha?" choked Miss Battle-Axe.

"Nose-picking?" gasped Miss Lovely.

"But what's the point of writing news
that everyone knows?" protested Horrid

Henry afterwards in Mrs. Oddbod's office. "News should be *new*."

Just wait until tomorrow's edition...

2

MOODY MARGARET'S SCHOOL

"Pay attention, Susan," shrieked Moody Margaret, "or you'll go straight to the principal."

"I *am* paying attention," said Sour Susan.

"This is boring," said Horrid Henry. "I want to play pirates."

"Silence," said Moody Margaret, whacking her ruler on the table.

"I want to be the teacher," said Susan.

"No," said Margaret.

"*I'll* be the teacher," said Horrid Henry. He'd send the class straight out for play-time, and tell them to run for their lives.

"Are you out of your mind?" snapped Margaret.

"Can I be the teacher?" asked Perfect Peter.

"NO!" shouted Margaret, Susan, and Henry.

"Why can't I be the principal?" said Susan sourly.

"Because," said Margaret.

"'cause why?" said Susan.

"'cause *I'm* the principal."

"But you're the principal *and* the teacher," said Susan. "It's not fair."

"It is too fair, 'cause you'd make a terrible principal," said Margaret.

"Would not!"

"Would too!"

"I think we should take turns being principal," said Susan.

"That," said Margaret, "is the dumbest idea I've ever heard. Do you see Mrs.

Oddbod taking *turns* being principal? I don't think so."

Margaret's class grumbled mutinously on the carpet inside the Secret Club tent.

"Class, I will now take roll," intoned Margaret. "Susan?"

"Here."

"Peter?"

"Here."

"Henry?"

"In the toilet."

Margaret scowled.

"We'll try that again. Henry?"

"Flushed away."

"Last chance," said Margaret severely. "Henry?"

"Dead."

Margaret made a big cross in her notebook.

"I will deal with you later."

"No one made *you* the big boss," muttered Horrid Henry.

"It's *my* house and we'll play what *I* want," said Moody Margaret. "And I want to play school."

Horrid Henry scowled. Whenever Margaret came to *his* house she was the guest and he had to play what *she* wanted. But whenever Henry went to her house Margaret was the boss 'cause it was *her* house. Ugggh. Why oh why did he have to live next door to Moody Margaret?

Mom had important work to do, and needed total peace and quiet, so Henry and Peter had been dumped at Margaret's. Henry had begged to go to Ralph's, but Ralph was visiting his grandparents. Now he was trapped all day with a horrible, moody old grouch. Wasn't it bad enough being with Miss Battle-Axe all week without having to spend his whole precious Saturday stuck at Margaret's? And, even worse, playing school?

"Come on, let's play pirates," said Henry. "I'm Captain Hook. Peter, walk the plank!"

"No," said Margaret. "I don't want to."

"But I'm the guest," protested Henry.

"So?" said Margaret. "This is *my* house and we play by *my* rules."

"Yeah, Henry," said Sour Susan.

"And I love playing school," said Perfect Peter. "It's such fun doing math."

Grrr. If only Henry could just go home. "I want a good report," Mom had said, "or you won't be going to Dave's bowling party tonight. It's very kind of Margaret and her mom to have you boys over to play."

"But I don't want to go to Margaret's!" howled Henry. "I want to stay home and watch TV!"

"N-O spells no," said Mom, and sent him kicking and screaming next door. "You can come home at five o'clock to get ready for Dave's party and not a minute before."

Horrid Henry gazed longingly over the wall. His house looked so inviting.

There was his bedroom window, twinkling at him. And his lonesome TV, stuck all by itself in the living room, just begging him to come over and turn it on. And all his wonderful toys, just waiting to be played with. Funny, thought Horrid Henry, his toys seemed so boring when he was in his room. But now that he was trapped at Margaret's, there was so much he longed to do at home.

Wait. He could hide out in his fort until five. Yes! Then he'd stroll into his house as if he'd been at Margaret's all day. But then Margaret's mom would be sure to call his mom to say that Henry had vanished and Henry would get into trouble. Big, big trouble. Big, big, banned from Dave's party trouble.

Or, he'd pretend to be sick. Margaret's mom was such an old fusspot she'd be sure to send him home immediately. Yippee. He was a genius. This would be easy. A few loud coughs, a few dramatic clutches at his stomach, a dash to the

bathroom, and he'd be sent straight home and...oops. He'd be put to bed. No party. No pizza. No bowling. And what was the point of pretending to be sick on the *weekend*? He was trapped.

Moody Margaret whacked her ruler on the table.

"I want everyone to write a story," said Margaret.

Write a story! Boy would Horrid Henry write a story. He seized a piece of paper and a pencil and scribbled away.

"Who'd like to read their story to the class?" said Margaret.

"I will," said Henry.

Once upon a time there was a moody old grouch named Margaret. Margaret had been born a frog but an ugly wizard cursed the frog and turned it into Margaret.

"That's enough, Henry," snapped Margaret. Henry ignored her.

"Ribbet ribbet," said Margaret Frog. "Ribbet ribbet ribbet." Everyone in the kingdom tried to get rid of this horrible croaking moody monster. But she smelled so awful that no one could get near her. And then one day a hero named Heroic Henry came, and he held his nose, grabbed the Margaret Monster and hurled her into outer space where she exploded and was never seen again.

THE END

Susan giggled. Margaret glared.

"F," said Margaret.

"Why?" said Horrid Henry innocently.

"'Cause," said Margaret. "I'm the teacher and I say it was boring."

"Did you think my story was boring, Peter?" demanded Henry.

Peter looked nervous.

"Did you?" said Margaret.

"Well, uhm, uhmm, I think mine is better," said Peter.

Once upon a time there was a dish towel named Terry. He was a very sad dish towel because he didn't have any dishes

to dry. One day he found a lot of wet dishes. Swish swish swish, they were dry in no time. "Yippee", said Terry the Towel, "I wonder when–"

"Boring!" shouted Horrid Henry.

"Excellent, Peter," said Moody Margaret. "*Much* better than Henry's."

Susan read a story about her cat.

My cat Kitty Kat is a big fat cat. She says meow. One day Kitty Kat met a dog. Meow, said Kitty Kat. Woof woof, said the dog. Kitty Kat ran away. So did the dog. The end.

"OK class, here are your scores," said Margaret. "Peter came in first."

"Yay!" said Perfect Peter.

"*What*?" said Susan. "My story was way better than his."

"Susan came in second, Henry came in ninth."

"How can I be ninth if there are only three people in the class?" demanded Horrid Henry.

"'Cause that's how bad your story was," said Margaret. "Now, I've made some worksheets for you. No talking or there'll be no break."

"Goody," said Perfect Peter. "I love worksheets. Are there lots of hard spelling words to learn?"

Horrid Henry had had enough. It was time to turn into Heroic Henry and destroy this horrible hag.

Henry crumpled up his worksheet and stood up.

"I've just been pretending to be a student," shouted Henry. "In fact, I'm a school inspector. And I'm shutting your school down. It's a disgrace."

Margaret gasped.

"You're a moody old grouch and you're a terrible teacher," said the inspector.

"I am not," said Margaret.

"She is not," said Susan.

"Silence when the inspector is speaking! You're the worst teacher I've ever seen. Imagine grading a stupid story about a tea towel higher than a fantastic tale about a wicked wizard."

"I'm the principal," said Margaret. "You can't boss me around."

"I'm the inspector," said Henry. "I can boss *everyone* around."

"Wrong, Henry," said Margaret, "because I'm the *chief* school inspector, and I'm inspecting *you*."

"Oh no you're not," said Henry.

"Oh yes I am," said Margaret.

"An inspector can't be a principal *and* a teacher, so there," said Henry.

"Oh yes I can," said Margaret.

"No you can't, 'cause I'm king and I sentence you to the Tower!" shrieked King Henry the Horrible.

"I'm the empress!" screamed Margaret. "Go to jail."

"I'm king of the universe, and I'm sending you to the snakepit," shrieked Henry.

"I'm queen of the universe and I'm going to chop off your head!"

"Not if I chop off yours first!" shrieked the king, yanking on the queen's hair.

The queen screamed and kicked the king.

The king screamed and kicked the queen.

"MOM!" screamed Margaret.

Margaret's mother rushed into the Secret Club tent.

"What's wrong with my little snugglechops?" said Margaret's mom.

"Henry's not playing my game," said Margaret. "And he kicked me."

"She kicked me first," said Henry.

"If you children can't play nicely I'll have to send you all home," said Margaret's mother severely.

"No!" said Peter.

Send him…home. Yes! Henry would make Margaret scream until the walls fell down. He would tell Margaret's mom her house smelled of pooh. He could… he would…

But if Henry was sent home for being horrid, Mom and Dad would be furious. There'd be no pizza and bowling party for sure.

Unless…unless…It was risky. It was dangerous. It could go horribly, horribly wrong. But desperate times call for desperate measures.

"Need a drink," said Henry, and ran out of the tent before Margaret could stop him.

Henry went into the kitchen to find Margaret's mom.

"I'm worried about Margaret, I think she's getting sick," said Henry.

"My little Maggie-muffin?" gasped Margaret's mom.

"She's being very strange," said Henry sadly. "She said she's the queen of the world and she would cut off my head."

"Margaret would *never* say such a thing," said her Mom. "She always plays beautifully. I've never seen a child so good at sharing."

Horrid Henry nodded. "I know. It must be 'cause she's sick. Maybe she caught something from Peter."

"Has Peter been ill?" said Margaret's mom. She looked pale.

"Oh yeah," lied Henry. "He's been throwing up, and—and—well, it's been awful. But I'm sure he's not *very* contagious."

"Throwing up?" said Margaret's mom weakly.

"And diarrhea," said Henry. "Tons and tons."

Margaret's mother looked ashen.

"Diarrhea?"

"But he's much better now," said Henry. "He's only run to the bathroom five times since we've been here."

Margaret's mother looked faint. "My little Margaret is so delicate…I can't risk…" she gasped. "I think you and Peter had better go home right away. Margaret! Margaret! Come in at once," she shouted.

Horrid Henry did not wait to be told twice. School was out!

Ahhhh, thought Horrid Henry happily, reaching for the TV remote, this was the life. Margaret had been sent to bed. He and Peter had been sent home. There was enough time to watch *Marvin the Maniac* and *Terminator Gladiator* before Dave's party.

"I can't help it that Margaret wasn't

feeling well, Mom," said Horrid Henry. "I just hope I haven't caught anything from *her*."

Honestly.

Mom was so selfish.

3

PERFECT PETER'S PIRATE PARTY

"Now, let's see," said Mom, consulting her list, "we need pirate flags, chocolate coins, swords, treasure chests, eyepatches, skull and crossbones plates. Have I missed anything?"

Horrid Henry stopped chewing. Wow! For once, Mom was talking about something important. His Purple Hand Pirate party wasn't till next month, but it was never too soon to start getting in supplies for the birthday party of the year. No, the century.

But wait. Mom had forgotten cutlasses. They were essential for the gigantic pirate battle Henry was planning. And what about all the ketchup for fake blood? And where were the buckets of sweets?

Horrid Henry opened his mouth to speak.

"That sounds great, Mom," piped Perfect Peter. "But don't forget the pirate napkins."

"Napkins. Check," said Mom, smiling.

Huh?

"I don't want napkins at my party," said Horrid Henry.

"This isn't for your party," said Mom. "It's for Peter's."

WHAT???

"What do you mean, it's for Peter's?" gasped Horrid Henry. He felt as if an icy hand had gripped him by the throat. He was having trouble breathing.

"Peter's birthday is next week, and he's having a pirate party," said Mom.

Perfect Peter kept eating his oatmeal.

"But he's having a Sammy the Snail party," said Horrid Henry, glaring at Peter.

"I changed my mind," said Perfect Peter.

"But pirates was *my* party idea!" shrieked Horrid Henry. "I've been planning it for months. You're just a copycat."

"You don't own pirates," said Peter. "Gordon had a pirate party for *his* birthday. So I want pirates for mine."

"Henry, you can still have a pirate party," said Dad.

"NOOOOOO!" screamed Horrid Henry. He couldn't have a pirate party *after* Peter. Everyone would think he'd copied his wormy toad brother.

Henry pounced. He was a poisoned arrow whizzing toward its target.

THUD! Peter fell off his chair.

SMASH! Peter's oatmeal bowl crashed to the floor.

"AAAEEEIIIII!" screeched Perfect Peter.

"Look what you've done, you horrid boy!" yelled Mom. "Say sorry to Peter."

"WAAAAAAAAAAA!" sobbed Peter.

"I won't!" said Horrid Henry. "I'm not sorry. He stole my party idea, and I hate him."

"Then go to your room and stay there," said Dad.

"It's not fair!" wailed Horrid Henry.

"What shall we do with the drunken sailor? What shall we do with the drunken sailor?" sang Perfect Peter as he walked past Henry's slammed bedroom door.

"Make him walk the plank!" screamed Horrid Henry. "Which is what will happen to you if you don't SHUT UP!"

"Mom! Henry told me to shut up," yelled Peter.

"Henry! Leave your brother alone," said Mom.

"You're the oldest. Can't you be grown-up for once and let him have his party in peace?" said Dad.

NO! thought Horrid Henry. He could not. He had to stop Peter having a pirate party. He just had to.

But how?

He could bribe Peter. But that would cost money that Henry didn't have. He could promise to be nice to him… No way. That was going too far. That little copycat worm did not deserve Henry's niceness.

Maybe he could *trick* him into abandoning his party idea. Hmmmm. Henry smiled. Hmmmmm.

Horrid Henry opened Peter's bedroom door and sauntered in. Perfect Peter was busy writing names on his YO HO HO pirate invitations. The same ones, Henry noticed, that *he'd* been planning to send,

with the peg-legged pirate swirling his cutlass and looking like he was about to leap out at you.

"You're supposed to be in your room," said Peter. "I'm telling on you."

"You know, Peter, I'm glad you're having a pirate party," said Henry.

Peter paused.

"You are?" said Peter cautiously.

"Yeah," said Horrid Henry. "It means you'll get the pirate cannibal curse and I won't."

"There's no such thing as a pirate cannibal curse," said Peter.

"Fine," said Horrid Henry. "Just don't blame me when you end up as a shrunken head dangling around a cannibal's neck."

Henry's such a liar, thought Peter. He's just trying to scare me.

"Gordon had a pirate party, and *he* didn't turn into a shrunken head," said Peter.

Henry sighed.

"Of course not, because his name doesn't start with P. The cannibal pirate who made the curse was named Blood Boil Bob. Look, that's him on the invitations," said Henry.

Peter glanced at the pirate. Was it his imagination, or did Blood Boil Bob have an especially mean and hungry look? Peter put down his crayon.

"He had a hateful younger brother named Paul, who became Blood Boil

54

Bob's first shrunken head," said Henry.
"Since then, the cannibal curse has
passed down to anyone else whose name
starts with P."

"I don't believe you, Henry," said
Peter. He was sure Henry was trying to
trick him. Lots of his friends had had
pirate parties, and none of them had
turned into a shrunken head.

On the other hand, none of his friends had names that began with P.

"How does the curse happen?" said Peter slowly.

Horrid Henry looked around. Then, putting a finger to his lips, he crept over to Peter's wardrobe and flung it open. Peter jumped.

"Just checking Blood Boil Bob's not in there," whispered Henry. "Now keep your voice down. Remember, dressing up as pirates, singing pirate songs, talking about treasure, wakes up the pirate cannibal. Sometimes— if you're lucky—he just steals all the treasure. Other times he… POUNCES," shrieked Henry.

Peter turned pale.

"Yo ho, yo ho, a pirate's life for me," sang Horrid Henry. "Yo ho—whoops, sorry, better not sing, in case *he* turns up."

"MOOOMMM!" wailed Peter. "Henry's trying to scare me!"

"What's going on?" said Mom.

"Henry said I'm going to turn into a shrunken head if I have a pirate party."

"Henry, don't be horrid," said Mom, glaring. "Peter, there's no such thing."

"Told you, Henry," said Perfect Peter.

"If I were you I'd have a Sammy the Slug party," said Horrid Henry.

"Sammy the *Snail*," said Peter. "I'm having a pirate party and you can't stop me. So there."

Rats, thought Horrid Henry. How could he make Peter change his mind?

"Don't **doooOOOO IT**, Peter," Henry howled spookily under Peter's door every night. "Beware! Beware!"

"Stop it, Henry!" screamed Peter.

"You'll be sorry," Horrid Henry

scrawled all over Peter's homework.

"Remember the cannibal curse," Henry whispered over supper the night before the party.

"Henry, leave your brother alone or you won't be coming to the party," said Mom.

What? Miss out on chocolate coins? Henry scowled. That was the least he was owed.

It was so unfair. Why did Peter have to wreck everything?

It was Peter's birthday party. Mom and Dad hung two huge skull and crossbones pirate flags outside the house. The exact ones, Horrid Henry noted bitterly, that he had planned for *his* birthday party. The cutlasses had been decorated and the galleon cake eaten. All that remained was for Peter's horrible guests, Tidy Ted, Spotless Sam, Goody-Goody Gordon, Perky Parveen, Helpful Hari, Tell-Tale Tim, and Mini Minnie to go on the treasure hunt.

"Yo ho, yo ho, a pirate's life for me," sang Horrid Henry. He was wearing his pirate skull scarf, his eyepatch, and his huge black skull and crossbones hat. His bloody cutlass gleamed.

"Don't sing that," said Peter.

"Why not, baby?" said Henry.

"You know why," muttered Peter.

"I warned you about Blood Boil Bob,

but you wouldn't listen," hissed Henry, "and now—" he drew his hand across his throat. "Hey everyone, let's play pin the tail on Peter."

"MOOOOOOOOMMMMMM!" wailed Peter.

"Behave yourself, Henry," muttered Mom, "or you won't be coming on the treasure hunt."

Henry scowled. The only reason he was even at this baby party was because the treasure chest was filled with chocolate coins.

Mom clapped her hands.

"Come on everyone, look for the clues hidden around the house to help you find the pirate treasure," she said, handing Peter a scroll. "Here's the first one."

Climb the stair,
if you dare,
you'll find a clue,
just for you.

"I found a clue," squealed Helpful Hari, grabbing the scroll dangling from the banister.

Turn to the left,
turn to the right,
reach into the bag,
don't get a fright.

The party pounded off to the left, then to the right, where another scroll hung in a pouch from Peter's doorknob.

"I found the treasure map!" shouted Perky Parveen.

"Oh goody," said Goody-Goody Gordon.

Everyone gathered round the ancient scroll.

"It says to go to the park," squealed Spotless Sam. "Look, X marks the spot where the treasure is buried."

Dad, waving a skull and crossbones flag, led the pirates out of the door and down the road to the park.

Horrid Henry ran ahead through the

park gates and took off his skull and crossbones hat and eyepatch. No way did he want anyone to think he was part of this *baby* pirate party. He glanced at the swings. Was there anyone here that he knew? Phew, no one, just some little girl on the slide.

The little girl looked up and stared at Horrid Henry. Horrid Henry stared back.

Uh oh.

Oh no.

Henry began to back away. But it was too late.

"Henwy!" squealed the little girl. "Henwy!"

It was Lisping Lily, New Nick's horrible sister. Henry had met her on the world's worst sleepover at Nick's house, where she—where she—

"Henwy! I love you, Henwy!" squealed

Lisping Lily, running toward him. "Will you marry with me, Henwy?"

Horrid Henry turned and ran down the winding path into the gardens. Lisping Lily ran after him. "Henwy! Henwy!"

Henry dived into some thick bushes and crouched behind them.

Please don't find me, please don't find me, he prayed.

Henry waited, his heart pounding. All he could hear was Peter's pirate party, advancing his way. Had he lost her?

"I think the treasure's over there!" shouted Peter.

Phew. He'd ditched her. He was safe.

"Henwy?" came a little voice. "Henwy! Where are you? I want to give you a big kiss."

AAAARRRGGHH!

Then Horrid Henry remembered who he was. The boy who'd got Miss Battle-

Axe sent to the principal. The boy who'd defeated the demon lunch lady. The boy who was scared of nothing (except shots). What was a pirate king like him doing hiding from some tiddly toddler?

Horrid Henry put on his pirate hat and grabbed his cutlass. He'd scare her off if it was the last thing he did.

"AAAAARRRRRRRRRRR!" roared the pirate king, leaping up and brandishing his bloody cutlass.

"AAAAAAAAAAAHHH!" squealed Lisping Lily. She turned and ran, crashing into Peter.

"Piwates! Piwates!" she screamed, dashing away.

Perfect Peter's blood ran cold. He looked into the thrashing bushes and saw a skull and crossbones rising out of the hedge, the gleam of sunlight on a blood-red cutlass…

"AAAAAAAHHHHHH!" screamed
Peter. "It's Blood Boil Bob!" He turned
and ran.

"AAAAAAAHHHHHH!" shrieked
Ted. He turned and ran.

"AAAAAAAHHHHHH!" shrieked
Gordon, Parveen, and the rest. They
turned and ran.

Huh? thought Horrid Henry, trying to
wriggle free.

Thud.

Henry's foot knocked against something hard. There, hidden beneath some leaves under the hedge, was a pirate chest.

Eureka!

"Help!" shrieked Perfect Peter. "Help! Help!"

Mom and Dad ran over.

"What's happened?"

"We got attacked by pirates!" wailed
Parveen.

"We ran for our lives!" wailed Gordon.

"Pirates?" said Mom.

"Pirates?" said Dad. "How many were
there?"

"Five!"

"Ten!"

"Hundreds!" wailed Mini Minnie.

"Don't be silly," said Mom.

"I'm sure they're gone now, so let's
find the treasure," said Dad.

Peter opened the map and headed for
the hedge nearest to the gate where the
treasure map showed a giant X.

"I'm too scared," he whimpered.

Helpful Hari crept to the treasure
chest and lifted the lid. Everyone gasped.
All that was left inside were a few
crumpled gold wrappers.

"The treasure's gone," whispered Peter.

Just then Horrid Henry sauntered along the path, twirling his hat.

"Where have you been?" said Mom.

"Hiding," said Horrid Henry truthfully.

"We got raided," gasped Ted.

"By pirates," gasped Gordon.

"No way," said Horrid Henry.

"They stole all the chocolate coins," wailed Peter.

Horrid Henry sighed.

"What did I tell you about the cannibal curse?" he said. "Just be glad you've still got your heads."

Hmmmm, boy, chocolate coins were always yummy, but raided chocolate coins tasted even better, thought Horrid Henry that night, shoving a few more candies into his mouth.

Come to think of it, there'd been too many pirate parties recently.

Now, a cannibal curse party…
Hmmmn.

4

HORRID HENRY ROBS THE BANK

"I want the skull!"

"I want the skull!"

"*I* want the skull!" said Horrid Henry, glaring.

"You had it last time, Henry," said Perfect Peter. "I *never* get it."

"Did not."

"Did too."

"*I'm* the guest so *I* get the skull," said Moody Margaret, snatching it from the box. "*You* can have the claw."

"NOOOOOOOO!" wailed Henry. "The skull is my lucky piece."

Margaret looked smug. "You know I'm going to win, Henry, 'cause I always do. So ha ha ha."

"Wanna bet?" muttered Horrid Henry.

The good news was that Horrid Henry was playing *Gotcha*, the world's best board game. Horrid Henry loved *Gotcha*. You rolled the dice and traveled round the board, collecting treasure, buying dragon lairs and praying you didn't land in your enemies' lairs or in the Dungeon.

The bad news was that Horrid Henry was having to play *Gotcha* with his worm toad crybaby brother.

The worst news was that Moody Margaret, the world's biggest cheater, was playing with them. Margaret's mom was out for the afternoon, and had dumped Margaret at Henry's. Why oh why did she have to play at his house?

Why couldn't her mom just dump her in the garbage where she belonged?

Unfortunately, the last time they'd played *Gotcha*, Margaret had won. The last two, three, four, and five times they'd played, Margaret had won. Margaret was a demon *Gotcha* player.

Well, not anymore.

This time, Henry was determined to beat her. Horrid Henry hated losing. By hook or by crook, he would triumph. Moody Margaret had beaten him at *Gotcha* for the very last time.

"Who'll be banker?" said Perfect Peter.

"Me," said Margaret.

"Me," said Henry. Being in charge of all the game's treasure was an excellent way of filling up your coffers when none of the other players was looking.

"I'm the guest so *I'm* banker," said Margaret. "You can be the dragon keeper."

Horrid Henry's hand itched to yank Margaret's hair. But then Margaret would scream and scream and Mom would send Henry to his room and

confiscate *Gotcha* until Henry was old and bald and dead.

"Touch any treasure that isn't yours, and you're dragon food," hissed Henry.

"Steal any dragon eggs that aren't yours and you're toast," hissed Margaret.

"If you're banker and Henry's the dragon keeper, what am I?" said Perfect Peter.

"A toad," said Henry. "And count yourself lucky."

Horrid Henry snatched the dice. "I'll go first." The player who went first always had the best chance of buying up the best dragon lairs like Eerie Eyrie and Hideous Hellmouth.

"No," said Margaret, "I'll go first."

"I'm the youngest, I should go first," said Peter.

"Me!" said Margaret, snatching the dice. "I'm the guest."

"Me!" said Henry, snatching them back.

"Me!" said Peter.

"MOM!" screamed Henry and Peter.

Mom ran in. "You haven't even started playing and already you're fighting," said Mom.

"It's my turn to go first!" wailed Henry, Margaret, and Peter.

"The rules say to roll the dice and whoever gets the highest number goes first," said Mom. "End of story." She left, closing the door behind her.

Henry rolled. Four. Not good.

"Peter's knee touched mine when I rolled the dice," protested Henry. "I get another turn."

"No you don't," said Margaret.

"Mooom! Henry's cheating!" shrieked Peter.

"If I get called one more time," screamed Mom from upstairs, "I will throw that game in the trash."

Eeeek.

Margaret rolled. Three.

"You breathed on me," hissed Margaret.

"Did not," said Henry.

"Did too," said Margaret. "I get another roll."

"No way," said Henry.

Peter picked up the dice.

"Low roll, low roll, low roll," chanted Henry.

"Stop it, Henry," said Peter.

"Low roll, low roll, low roll," chanted Henry louder.

Peter rolled an eleven.

"Yippee, I go first," trilled Peter.

Henry glared at him.

Perfect Peter took a deep breath, and rolled the dice to start the game.

Five. A Fate square.

Perfect Peter moved his gargoyle to the Fate square and picked up a Fate card. Would it tell him to claim a treasure hoard, or send him to the Dungeon? He squinted at it.

"The og…the ogr…I can't read it," he said. "The words are too hard for me."

Henry snatched the card. It read:

***The Ogres make you king for a day.
Collect 20 rubies from the other players.***

"The Ogres make you king for a day. Give 20 rubies to the player on your left," read Henry. "And that's me, so pay up."

Perfect Peter handed Henry twenty rubies.

Tee hee, thought Horrid Henry.

"I think you read that Fate card wrong, Henry," said Moody Margaret grimly.

Uh oh. If Margaret read Peter the card, he was dead. Mom would make them stop playing, and Henry would get into trouble. Big, big trouble.

"Did not," said Henry.

"Did too," said Margaret. "I'm telling on you."

Horrid Henry looked at the card again. "Whoops. Silly me. I read it too fast," said Henry. "It says, give 20 rubies to *all* the other players."

"Thought so," said Moody Margaret.

Perfect Peter rolled the dice. Nine! Oh no, that took Peter straight to Eerie Eyrie, Henry's favorite lair. Now Peter could buy it. Everyone always landed on it and had to pay a ransom or get eaten. Rats, rats, rats. "1, 2, 3, 4, 5, 6, 7, 8, 9, look, Henry, I've landed on Eerie Eyrie and no one owns it yet," said Peter.

"Don't buy it," said Henry. "It's the worst lair on the board. No one ever lands on it. You'd just be wasting your money."

"Oh," said Peter. He looked doubtful.

"But...but..." said Peter.

"Save your money for when you land in other people's lairs," said Henry. "That's what I'd do."

"OK," said Peter, "I'm not buying."

Tee hee.

Henry rolled. Six. Yes! He landed on Eerie Eyrie. "I'm buying it!" crowed Henry.

"But Henry," said Peter, "you just told me not to buy it."

"You shouldn't listen to me," said Henry.

"MOM!" wailed Peter.

Soon Henry owned Eerie Eyrie, Gryphon Gulch, and Creepy Hollow, but he was dangerously low on treasure. Margaret owned Rocky Ravine, Vulture Valley, and Hideous Hellmouth.

Margaret kept her treasure in her treasure pouch, so it was impossible to see how much money she had, but Henry guessed she was also low.

Peter owned Demon Den and one dragon egg. Margaret was stuck in the

Dungeon. Yippee! This meant if Henry landed on one of her lairs he'd be safe. Horrid Henry rolled, and landed on Vulture Valley, guarded by a baby dragon.

"Gotcha!" shrieked Margaret. "Gimme 25 rubies."

"You're in the Dungeon, you can't collect ransom," said Henry. "Nah nah ne nah nah!"

"Can too!"

"Cannot!"

"That's how we play at *my* house," said Margaret.

"In case you hadn't noticed, we're not *at* your house," said Henry.

"But I'm the guest," said Margaret. "Gimme my money!"

"No!" shouted Henry. "You can't just make up rules."

"The rules say…" began Perfect Peter.

"Shut up, Peter!" screamed Henry and Margaret.

"I'm not paying," said Henry.

Margaret glowered. "I'll get you for this, Henry," she hissed.

It was Peter's turn. Henry had just upgraded his baby dragon guarding Eerie Eyrie to a big, huge, fire-breathing, slavering monster dragon. Peter was

only five squares away. If Peter landed there, he'd be out of the game.

"Land! Land! Land! Land! Land!" chanted Henry. "Yum yum yum, my dragon is just waiting to eat you up."

"Stop it, Henry," said Peter. He rolled. Five.

"Gotcha!" shouted Horrid Henry. "I own Eerie Eyrie! You've landed in my lair, pay up! That's 100 rubies."

"I don't have enough money," wailed Perfect Peter.

Horrid Henry drew his finger across his throat.

"You're dead meat, worm,"
he chortled.

Perfect Peter burst
into tears and ran out
of the room.

"Waaaaaaahhhhh,"
he wailed. "I lost!"

Horrid Henry glared at Moody
Margaret.

Moody Margaret glared at Horrid
Henry.

"You're next to be eaten," snarled
Margaret.

"*You're* next," snarled Henry.

Henry peeked under the *Gotcha* board
where his treasure was hidden. Oh no.
Not again. He'd spent so much on
dragons he was down to his last few
rubies. If he landed on any of Margaret's
lairs, he'd be wiped out. He had to get

more treasure. He had to. Why oh why had he let Margaret be banker?

His situation was desperate. Peter was easy to steal money from, but Margaret's eagle eyes never missed a trick. What to do, what to do? He had to get more treasure, he had to.

And then suddenly Horrid Henry had a brilliant, spectacular idea. It was so brilliant that Henry couldn't believe he'd never thought of it before. It was dangerous. It was risky. But what choice did he have?

"I need to go to the bathroom," said Henry.

"Hurry up," said Margaret, scowling.

Horrid Henry dashed to the downstairs bathroom…and sneaked straight out the back door. Then he jumped over the garden wall and crept into Margaret's house.

Quickly he ran to her living room and scanned her games cupboard. Aha! There was Margaret's *Gotcha*.

Horrid Henry stuffed his pockets with treasure. He stuffed more under his shirt and in his socks.

"Is that you, my little sugarplum?" came a voice from upstairs. "Maggie Moo-Moo?"

Henry froze. Margaret's mom was home.

"Maggie Plumpykins," cooed her mom, coming down the stairs. "Is that you—oooo?"

"No," squeaked Henry. "I mean,

yes," he squawked. "Got to go back to Henry's, 'bye!"

And Horrid Henry ran for his life.

"You took a long time," said Margaret.

Henry hugged his stomach.

"Upset tummy," he lied. Oh boy was he brilliant. Now, with tons of cash which he would slip under the board, he was sure to win.

Henry picked up the dice and handed them to Margaret.

"Your turn," said Henry.

Henry's hungry dragon stood waiting six places away in Goblin Gorge.

Roll a six, roll a six, roll a six, prayed Horrid Henry.

Not a six, not a six, not a six, prayed Moody Margaret.

Margaret rolled. Four. She moved her skull to the Haunted Forest.

"Your turn," said Margaret.

Henry rolled a three. Oh no. He'd landed on Hideous Hellmouth, where Margaret's giant dragon loomed.

"Yes!" squealed Margaret. "Gotcha! You're dead! Ha ha hahaha, I won!" Moody Margaret leaped to her feet and did a victory dance, whooping and cheering.

Horrid Henry smiled at her.

"Oh dear," said Horrid Henry. "Oh dearie, dearie me. Looks like I'm dragon food—NOT!"

"What do you mean, not?" said

Margaret. "You're dead meat, you can't pay me."

"Not so fast," said Horrid Henry. With a flourish he reached under the board and pulled out a pile of treasure.

"Let me see, 100 rubies, is it?" said Henry, counting off a pile of coins.

Margaret's mouth dropped open.

"How did you…what…how…huh?" she spluttered.

Henry shrugged modestly. "Some of us know how to play this game," he said. "Now roll."

Moody Margaret rolled and landed on a Fate square.

Go straight to Eerie Eyrie, read the card.

"Gotcha!" shrieked Horrid Henry. He'd won!! Margaret didn't have enough money to stop being eaten. She was dead. She was doomed.

"I won! I won! You can't pay me, nah nah ne nah nah," shrieked Horrid Henry, leaping up and doing a victory dance. "I am the *Gotcha* king!"

"Says who?" said Moody Margaret, pulling a handful of treasure from her pouch.

Huh?

"You stole that money!" spluttered Henry. "You stole the bank's money. You big fat cheater."

"Did not."

"Did too."

"CHEATER!" howled Moody Margaret.

"CHEATER!" howled Horrid Henry.

Moody Margaret grabbed the board and hurled it to the floor.

"I won," said Horrid Henry.

"Did not."

"Did too, Maggie Moo-Moo."

"Don't call me that," said Margaret, glaring.

"Call you what, Moo-Moo?"

"I challenge you to a re-match," said Moody Margaret.

"You're on," said Horrid Henry.

Acknowledgments

Special thanks to Hannah, Archie, and Rufus Kempton for telling me all about pirate parties and Michael McIntyre for sharing his board-game winning strategies.

About the Author

Photo: Francesco Guidicini

Francesca Simon spent her childhood on the beach in California and then went to Yale and Oxford Universities to study medieval history and literature. She now lives in London with her family. She has written over forty-five books and won the Children's Book of the Year in 2008 at the Galaxy British Book Awards for *Horrid Henry and the Abominable Snowman*.